The Further Adventures of Aladdin

Aladdin

4 Iago's Promise

BY A. R. Plumb

ILLUSTRATED BY
Laureen Burger
Mark Marderosian
H. R. Russell

DISNEY
PRESS
NEW YORK

Look for all the books in this series:
#1 A Thief in the Night
#2 Birds of a Feather
#3 A Small Problem
#4 Iago's Promise

Library of Congress Catalog Card Number: 94-72229
ISBN: 0-7868-4024-2
FIRST EDITION
1 3 5 7 9 10 8 6 4 2

Disney's
The Further Adventures of
Aladdin
4 Iago's Promise

Abu scampered up the trunk of the tallest palm tree in the palace gardens. Directly below him was a birdbath. The little monkey pulled a ripe red tomato from under his fez. Then he settled down to wait. He knew Iago would be coming out for his morning bath any minute now.

While he waited, Abu examined the bare spot on his long tail. Yesterday a certain parrot — a certain parrot named *Iago* — had glued Abu's tail to a chair. When Abu had yanked his tail free, some of the fur had come off.

But Iago was going to get what was coming to him now.

At that moment the sound of loud, off-key humming filled the air. *Iago!* Abu ducked out of sight behind a palm frond.

Iago zoomed around the tree. He perched on the edge of his little round birdbath. Then he stuck one toe in the water. "That's a little cold," he muttered to himself. "I'm not saying it's ice water or anything. But a guy could definitely catch a cold in that water."

With a sigh, Iago hopped into the water. He shivered and flapped his wings. "And I could use some bubbles," he added. "Would it kill anyone if I had a few bubbles?"

He quickly finished his bath. Then he fluttered his wings to shake off the water. "Now for breakfast," he said. "I hope it's not more of that slimy oatmeal we had yesterday. I'm thinking more along the lines of a nice ripe piece of fruit."

Abu aimed his tomato and grinned. Iago wanted something ripe? Well, he was going to get it.

Splat! The tomato landed right on Iago's head. It dribbled into his eyes and over his beak.

"Hey!" Iago shouted. He glared up into the tree.

Abu stamped his feet and laughed.

"You!" Iago cried. "As if I couldn't guess. You puny primate! What the heck did you do that for?"

Abu grabbed his tail and shook the bare patch.

"That was just a little joke," Iago said. "A harmless prank. Gluing a monkey's tail to furniture, now *that's* funny. Tomatoes on the head, that's *not* funny." He tried to wipe the mess off his head. Tomato pulp slid down his back and landed with a splash in the birdbath.

Abu laughed even harder.

"That does it!" Iago cried, taking off and zooming toward Abu. "This time you've had it, monkey boy! Just wait until I get my wings around your scrawny little neck. Then we'll see how hard you're laughing!"

Abu scampered to the end of a palm frond and jumped through an open palace window. He ran downstairs and hid behind the Sultan's golden throne.

A second later Iago charged into the throne room. Abu crouched low.

"What's the matter, Iago?" asked Aladdin, Abu's best friend. He was working at a desk in the throne room with Princess

Jasmine. The Sultan was watching them from his throne.

"What's the matter?" Iago exclaimed. "That little flea merchant, that undersize gorilla, that walking hairball, that —"

Aladdin grinned. "Let me guess. You must be talking about Abu."

"Who else could I be talking about?" Iago cried. "He hit me with a tomato. Correction. He hit me with a *dozen* tomatoes!"

"Didn't you glue his tail to a chair yesterday?" Aladdin asked.

"Maybe," Iago said. "But that was only because the day before he put molasses in my bed."

"And the day before that? Didn't you do something to him?"

Iago hesitated. "Hold on, I'm thinking here."

"Maybe I can help," Jasmine said. "Do you remember hiding lizards in Abu's fez?"

"Hey, he had it coming," Iago grumbled. "He ought to be glad they weren't cobras."

"Well, you two will have to solve this little disagreement yourselves," Aladdin said.

5

"We have more important things to worry about. We have to finalize the plans for the Ceremony of Fireworks. It's tomorrow night — that's less than two days away, you know."

"And that's more important than the monkey nearly killing me? I'm telling you, he dropped an entire crate of tomatoes on me! I could have been crushed. Pulverized. Tomato-parrot soup."

"Mmm," said the Sultan, rubbing his stomach. "Speaking of soup, what do you think we'll be having for lunch today?"

Iago sighed loudly. "It's pathetic, I tell you. I can't even take my morning bath in peace." Suddenly his eyes lit up. "Wait a minute. Wait just a minute here! I'm having a brainstorm. Which is not easy when you've just been bombarded by a thousand vegetables." He flew over and perched on Aladdin's shoulder. "I want a new birdbath! That's what I need. A new birdbath, with a roof over it so the little beast can't attack me."

"Iago," Aladdin said, "we don't have time for your whining and complaining."

"Whining! Complaining! I never complain. I ask you, who has *ever* heard me complain?" Iago asked.

Aladdin raised his hand. So did Jasmine. So did the Sultan. Even Abu stepped out of his hiding place behind the throne to raise his hand.

"Okay, maybe once or twice I might have complained." Iago shrugged. "But I never whine."

"You complain constantly," Aladdin said. "You whine about everything."

"If I had a new birdbath with a roof, I wouldn't have to complain," Iago said. He thought for a moment. "I'm seeing marble, a little carving, a few decorations, some paintings. . . . Maybe a painting of me! Yes, that would be nice."

"Iago," said Jasmine, "we really don't have time for this."

"Fine, no time for poor Iago. Forget Iago. That misbehaving monkey can dump almost a billion hard tomatoes, plus some rocks . . . yes, I think there were definitely rocks involved —"

Jasmine sighed and rolled her eyes. "Iago, if you think you can whine your way into a new birdbath, forget it. We're not falling for it."

"Hold on." Aladdin snapped his fingers. "I think I've got it! We'll see about getting you that new birdbath, Iago."

"Finally," said Iago, giving Jasmine a triumphant look. "The kid sees reason."

"But," Aladdin added with a smile, "it comes with one big condition."

"Condition?" Iago asked. "Sure, gimme a condition, any condition. Just as long as I can take a bath without monkey boy turning it into a vegetable dip."

"Okay then. Here's the condition," Aladdin said. "You can't complain or say anything unkind about anyone for a week."

Jasmine laughed. "Great idea, Aladdin!" She shook her head. "But a week is too long. He'll explode if he has to be nice for a whole week. Let's make it until the Ceremony."

"All I gotta do is not complain for two days?" Iago asked.

"Not a *single* mean word until the fireworks start," Jasmine said.

Iago considered. "Suppose the ape gets on my nerves?"

"Suffer in silence," said Aladdin.

"Suppose he pulls a stunt like he did with the tomatoes?"

"Then you'll just have to grin and bear it," Jasmine advised. "If you can do that, you'll get your new birdbath."

"Okay then. No sweat," said Iago. "My beak is sealed."

Abu started laughing. He stuck out his tongue at Iago.

"Can it, banana breath," Iago snapped.

"Iago!" Jasmine warned.

"What? Oh, that. That was just a term of endearment," Iago said. He patted Abu on the head. "See? Best buddies."

Just then a tall, thin man marched into the throne room. He was dressed in the uniform of the palace guard. "Er, hello there. Do I know you?" asked the Sultan uncertainly.

The man bowed low. "My name is Sargon, Your Highness," he said. "I am filling in for Rasoul, the head of your palace guard."

Aladdin frowned. "Who assigned you to that position?"

"Rasoul himself," Sargon answered. "Before this, I headed the guard of the great Sultan of Aquitar." He handed the Sultan an envelope. "Here is my letter of recommendation."

The Sultan scanned the note. "Ah, well, everything seems to be in order. By the way, what's the matter with Rasoul?"

"He broke his leg," Sargon said. "He had a most unfortunate accident. It seems he fell down the flight of stairs leading to the treasure room."

"I thought I saw a carpenter working on those stairs this morning," said Jasmine.

"As it happens, that is my brother, Jah-

mad," said Sargon. "The finest craftsman in all the desert."

"Oh yes, that's right. I've asked him to do some work around the old place," said the Sultan. "Next he's going to enlarge my throne a bit. Strangest thing, the way it keeps shrinking."

"Oh yeah, right. Blame it on the throne," Iago whispered. Aladdin sent him a warning look. Iago smiled sheepishly. Then his eyes lit up. "Hey!" he said to Sargon.

"Maybe your brother could help me out with a little redecorating project."

"Not so fast, Iago," Aladdin said. "The Ceremony is two whole days away."

"Perhaps your little feathered friend needs a new cage?" Sargon asked Aladdin.

"Cage!" Iago squawked. "Don't go using the *C*-word around here, bozo!"

"Watch it, Iago," Jasmine scolded. "This is your last warning. I mean it."

"Oops." Iago gave a shrug. "I *meant* to say bozo, *sir.*"

"So, Sargon, do you know about the Ceremony of Fireworks?" Aladdin asked.

A shadow of a smile passed over Sargon's lips. "Rasoul explained a great deal. He said we should expect a huge crowd in front of the palace at dusk for the fireworks display."

"The Ceremony is an Agrabah tradition," said the Sultan excitedly. "I always get to set off the very first firecracker!"

"And where will these fireworks be stored?" Sargon asked.

"We keep them in a cool place," said Aladdin. "The storage room in the west wing. Right next to the treasure room."

"Ah, yes." Sargon nodded. "In Rasoul's absence, I've volunteered to watch the treasure room myself during the festivities. You can't be too careful, with all the crowds."

"Good thinking," said the Sultan.

"Will that be all?" asked Sargon. "I must go check with my brother to see how he's progressing on those repairs."

"See if he can fit in a birdbath when he's done," Iago said. "I'm thinking maybe a fountain. One of those fish fountains, you know what I'm saying? The kind that spit out water?"

"Don't mind Iago, Sargon," said Jasmine with a laugh. "I doubt he'll be needing your brother's services."

"We'll just see about that," said Iago as he watched Sargon depart. "For the next two days, this parrot's going to be a total pussycat."

"Maybe I'll just go have a little talk with that carpenter myself," Iago muttered as he flew out of the throne room a few minutes later. "He might as well get started on my birdbath right away. It's not like I can't be nice for a couple of days. Beneath these feathers lies a heart of gold. Okay, a heart of silver, maybe. Of brass. Concrete. Okay, so I'm not exactly Mr. Congeniality. That doesn't mean I can't keep my mouth shut."

Iago turned down the long hallway that led to the treasure room. He spotted Sargon standing near the stairway at the end of the hall. The guard was talking in a hushed voice to a man with a hammer.

"That's gotta be his brother," Iago said as he flew closer.

"How are the repairs going on that broken stair?" Sargon was asking Jahmad.

"Almost finished," said Jahmad. He was a short, pudgy man with tiny eyes. "I can't imagine what happened to it!"

"Perhaps it was those nails someone pried loose?" Sargon said with a dark laugh.

Iago froze. He flattened himself against a peacock statue. "Am I hearing things or did that sound suspicious?" he whispered to himself.

"Poor Rasoul." Sargon clucked his tongue. "Breaking his leg at such an unfortunate time. Good thing I had that letter of recommendation from the Sultan of Aquitar."

"Good thing I'm an excellent forger," Jahmad replied with a laugh.

Iago's eyes widened. Forger? "I *know* that sounds suspicious!" he whispered. Iago gulped. What were Jahmad and Sargon

planning? Whatever it was, there was only one thing to do. Iago had to tell Aladdin what was going on. What a shame. Jahmad could have built Iago a wonderful birdbath. And now Iago was going to have to turn him in. He tiptoed around the corner and headed toward the throne room.

Then he stopped. "Wait a minute!" he exclaimed. He had just remembered — he had promised not to say a mean word about anyone for two whole days. And saying that someone was a liar and a forger was not exactly nice.

Iago scratched his head. Of course, it wasn't as though he had any *real* proof about Jahmad and Sargon. Maybe he'd misunderstood them. Yeah. That was it. He'd just jumped to conclusions. Silly Iago, always thinking the worst about people. So what if Sargon had a nasty cackle and a whiny voice? Maybe it was a family trait. Everyone in Iago's family had a gruff voice. Even his grandmother. And so what if Jahmad had beady little eyes? Come to think of it, Iago had beady little eyes, too.

Just then Iago heard a familiar chitter. He turned and saw Abu at the other end of the hall. The little monkey pointed at Iago.

"What's peanut breath up to now?" Iago muttered.

Suddenly Rajah, Princess Jasmine's tiger, galloped around the corner at top speed. He raced up and planted his huge, furry paws on either side of Iago. The whole hall shuddered with the tiger's fierce roar.

Abu clapped his hands and laughed.

"What did that poor excuse for a rodent tell you?" Iago asked in a nervous chirp. "Whatever it is, he's lying. Ya gotta believe me."

Rajah sniffed. He licked his chops.

"Are those capped?" Iago asked, gulping. "I mean, those are some nice-looking fangs. Who's your dentist, anyway?"

Rajah snapped at Iago. Iago shot up into the air and flapped with all his might. "I'll get you for this, monkey boy!" he yelled as he tore down the hall.

Iago swooped out the nearest door and headed into the palace gardens. Rajah was still right behind him. The tiger leaped in the air and nipped at Iago's tail feathers. Abu followed, howling with laughter.

The Genie and Carpet were playing croquet on the wide lawn. Iago circled them. "Guys, ya gotta help me here," he cried.

"Hold that thought," said the Genie. He aimed his mallet at a yellow ball. "I'm finally about to beat the rug at something."

Suddenly Rajah swiped at Iago with his

huge paw and pulled him to the ground. *SPLAT!* Iago was trapped beneath the tiger's paw. "The cat is drooling, guys!" Iago screeched. "I could use a little backup, pronto!"

The Genie hit the croquet ball, but it just missed the wicket. Carpet patted him on the back. The Genie groaned. "Okay, so you won this game, Carpet, my man," he said. "But I've got just one word for you — *tiddlywinks.*"

Rajah licked his chops and leaned a little closer to Iago.

"This is not good," Iago cried. "I'm saying this is definitely a not-good situation I am in! Yoo-hoo! Big blue magic man over there! Do you think maybe you could interrupt your game long enough to save a poor defenseless birdie?"

The Genie put down his croquet mallet. He looked over at Rajah and Iago. "Hmm," he said. "Judging by the tiger's expression, I'd guess that the princess forgot to put out the kitty chow this morning."

Even Abu looked a little worried. He tapped Rajah on the shoulder and shook his head.

"See? Even peanut brain sees the error of his ways," Iago said. "I'm innocent, I tell you! Genie, zap me already!"

"Well, as you know, ever since Al freed me, my powers are just *semi*phenomenal and *nearly* cosmic," the Genie said. "But I'll give it a whirl. What's the worst that could happen?"

Poof! Suddenly Rajah was twenty times his old size. He towered over the others. When he flicked his tail, the ground shuddered like an earthquake.

"Whoopsie," said the Genie. "Looks like we're having ourselves a little *cat*astrophe."

"Great. Stupendous. Stop the presses," Iago moaned from beneath Rajah's giant paw. "I am now officially a dead duck."

Zap! Before Iago could say another word, the Genie turned Rajah back into his old self.

At that very moment Jasmine appeared in the gardens. "Iago!" she called. "Where are you hiding? What were you thinking, taking my bubble bath?"

"Princess!" Iago called. "I'm over here, Princess! And what is this, blame the bird day? I didn't take your bubbles!"

Jasmine knelt down to stroke Rajah's head. He purred contentedly. "By the way, don't eat Iago, Rajah," she said calmly. "It isn't polite. Even if his birdbath *is* filled with my bubbles."

"I'm innocent, I tell you!" Iago screeched. "Now get this stupid monster to let me go before I become a between-meals snack." He shook his wings in disgust. "I mean, look at this! He's drooling on me!"

Abu started to laugh. Jasmine turned to look at the monkey suspiciously. Abu gulped. He gave Jasmine a guilty smile and backed up a few steps.

"Abu," Jasmine scolded. "That wasn't nice!"

"Nice! Nice is not the half of it!" Iago cried. He pointed a wing at Abu. "The monkey did it! I was framed! It's a setup!"

"Rajah, let Iago go," Jasmine said. "He didn't steal the bubble bath. It was Abu."

With a sigh, Rajah lifted his paw.

"Phew!" Iago got up and smoothed his feathers. He shook a wing at Rajah. "I've got one word for you, tuna breath. Mouth-wash!" Iago spun around to face Abu. "And as for you . . . just wait until I tell Aladdin what you've been up to! You'll be a monkey-fur sweater by the time I'm through with you!"

"Iago," Jasmine said, "I know you're upset —"

"Upset! *Upset!* News flash, Princess. This is not upset. This is way, way beyond upset. This is —"

"Have you forgotten our deal?" Jasmine asked. "Really, Iago, it's only been twenty minutes. I was hoping you could last a little longer."

"But . . . but I was framed! Bamboozled by that traitorous chump of a chimp! You can't expect me to let this go. I'm covered with cat slobber!"

"Try a little patience, Iago," Jasmine said. "It was just a harmless prank." She stroked Rajah's back. "And by the way, my tiger doesn't slobber."

Iago opened his mouth to protest. After all, he had the evidence on his side — he was covered with tiger drool.

But Jasmine shook her finger at him. "Two days of niceness, Iago," she said. "I know you can do it."

Iago sputtered. He crossed his wings and glared at Abu. Abu grinned.

"I want golden faucets," Iago said at last. "And marble carvings. And my very own supply of bubble bath."

"We'll see," Jasmine said with a smile. "It all depends on how well you behave."

"Behave, she says," Iago muttered. He walked over to Rajah. Nervously he stroked the tiger's head. Then he went over to Abu. Abu ducked, but it was too late. Iago planted a great big wet kiss on the monkey's face.

"What a beautiful moment," the Genie

said. He zapped up a handful of handker-
chiefs and gave one to Jasmine and one to
Carpet. Then he blew his own nose with a
loud honk.

"Yeah, beautiful," Iago said sarcastically.
"I'm all choked up." He scowled at Abu.
"But once those fireworks go off and I've
got my birdbath, chimp, it's open season.
Consider yourself warned."

Iago stared at his reflection in his birdbath and made a face. "You miserable ugly knobby-kneed wart-infested sand buzzard," he muttered. "You —"

"Iago?" Jasmine asked as she strolled past. "What are you doing?"

"Uh, well, you see, Princess . . ." Iago cleared his throat. "I was just letting off some steam, if you know what I mean. It's been twenty-four hours of happy-face Iago, and I'm telling you, I'm going to explode if I don't say something mean to *some*body."

"One more day, Iago," Jasmine reminded him. "Come on, you can do it."

"No, I can't," Iago said with a sigh. "I don't know how much longer I can hold it in. I gotta be me, Princess."

"I'll let you in on a little secret," Jasmine said. "Aladdin is planning to talk to Jahmad today about your birdbath — just in case you actually pull off this little bet."

Iago considered. "You think I can do it?"

"While I'm at it, I'll tell you another secret," Jasmine said. "Deep down inside you, I really think there lurks a heart of gold." She paused, frowning. "Well, silver, anyway."

Iago watched her walk away. Maybe Jasmine was right. Why, he had only eleven hours, seventeen minutes, and thirty-two more seconds left of niceness. *Then* he could go back to being his rotten, nasty, lovable self again.

Maybe he'd just go see if Jahmad and Aladdin had worked up any details on the birdbath yet. He hoped Aladdin hadn't forgotten to mention the fish fountain.

Iago flew into the palace. He headed toward the hall where he'd seen Jahmad fixing the step leading down to the treasure room the day before. Jahmad's big wooden toolbox sat at the top of the stairs. But there was no sign of Jahmad himself.

Just then Iago heard a door creak. It was the door to the storage room halfway down the hall. Iago hid behind a statue and watched as Sargon stuck his head out.

When he'd made sure the coast was clear, Sargon tiptoed out of the storage room with Jahmad on his heels. They were carrying something in their arms. Iago had to peer around the statue to see what they were holding.

Fireworks! Sargon and Jahmad were stealing fireworks! But why?

"Our plan is complete," said Sargon. "The only remaining obstacle was finding a way to open the treasure room door." He

frowned. "I still can't believe that rotten Rasoul wouldn't give me the key."

"It doesn't matter. Now we have the solution," Jahmad said. "The big, *loud* solution."

So *that's* what the fireworks are for, Iago thought. Sargon and Jahmad were going to blow open the treasure room door during the Ceremony and steal the Sultan's jewels. Iago had been right about them all along!

He watched as the two men deposited the fireworks in Jahmad's big toolbox, then closed the lid and locked it. Iago gulped. There was no way he could keep pretending that everything was okay. Everything was definitely *not* okay.

With a deep sigh, Iago flew down the hall to the throne room. An annoying little voice in his head was telling him he had to warn someone about Sargon and Jahmad — and fast.

Iago found the Sultan in the throne room. He was getting up out of his throne, then sitting down, over and over again.

"Uh, pardon me, O Mighty Guy, but what's the deal?" Iago asked. "Playing musical throne?"

"Jahmad, that wonderful carpenter, enlarged my throne this morning," the Sultan exclaimed. "It's a miracle! I feel a hundred pounds lighter!"

Iago started to laugh, but he managed to turn it into a cough. "Um, and you look it, too, if I may say so," he said, trying to muster up some enthusiasm.

"My, you *have* gotten nicer," said the Sultan. "I've always said that beneath those feathers lies a heart of gold." He considered for a moment. "Well, silver, anyway."

Iago perched on one arm of the throne. "So this Jahmad guy's an okay carpenter?" he asked.

"Yes, indeed. He'll be making you a splendid birdbath," said the Sultan. "That is, of course," he added with a chuckle, "if you can actually be nice for the rest of the day."

Iago sighed. "You didn't notice anything,

well, a little strange about that Jahmad guy and his brother?"

"Strange?"

"Well, they do both have a nasty sneer, for one thing. And Sargon has that whiny voice. And that Jahmad has the beadiest little eyes —"

"So do you," the Sultan pointed out.

"Thank you," Iago said. "The thing is, see, I overheard those guys talking, and, well, I don't want to sound suspicious or anything, but there's something rotten about them —"

"Now, now!" the Sultan said quickly. He put his hands over his ears. "Careful, Iago!

I don't want to have to tell Aladdin and Jasmine that you've broken your promise."

"But what I'm trying to do here is maybe prevent some trouble," Iago said. "Ya gotta believe me — "

"Why is it you always see the worst in people?" the Sultan asked. "Jahmad is a wonderful carpenter. Sargon is a loyal guard. And you're twelve hours away from a beautiful new birdbath, Iago! Don't ruin it."

"Eleven hours, fourteen minutes, and twelve seconds," said Iago glumly. "But who's counting?"

"Now, not another word about this," the Sultan said. "And that's an order."

"Sure, Your Royalness," Iago replied. "Your wish is my command and all that."

He left the throne room and flew into the main hall. There he found Aladdin talking to Jahmad. They were looking at a big piece of paper with line drawings on it.

Iago paused. That annoying little voice

was nagging him again. "Man, I *hate* that voice," he muttered.

With a sigh, he flew over to Aladdin and perched on his shoulder. "We gotta talk," Iago said. "In private. Now, before I talk myself out of talking."

"Iago, I'm a little busy here," Aladdin said.

"It's important," Iago whispered in his ear. "The future of the kingdom could be at stake."

Aladdin rolled his eyes. "Can you excuse me for a minute, Jahmad?" he asked. He walked over to a corner, with Iago still on his shoulder. "So what's the big emergency?"

"Well, the thing is, I'm not so sure about that guy," Iago said, pointing to Jahmad. "I'm worried that maybe — "

"Don't say it," Aladdin interrupted. "I know what's on your mind."

"You do?" Iago asked, relieved.

"Sure. And you can relax. Jahmad is really a fantastic carpenter. We were just looking at some drawings he made up for your birdbath."

"My . . ."

"Yeah, well, you were so good yesterday, I figured you might actually have a shot at pulling it off." He shook one finger at Iago playfully. "But be careful. We're going to be watching you. One slip and you're stuck with your old birdbath for good."

Iago thought for a moment. Maybe, just maybe, he was wrong about Sargon and Jahmad. And even if he *was* right, what were the odds that those two bozos could really pull off a heist during the Ceremony, right under the nose of the Sultan's guards? Maybe Iago could just keep an eye on the brothers before the Ceremony. That way he could step in when and if it seemed necessary and save the day himself.

Besides, if he mentioned his suspicions, he'd lose his chance at the birdbath. He could already imagine the fish fountain splashing gently on his wings. He could see his gorgeous face reflected in the mirrors.

He could picture the golden roof . . . the
roof that would keep tomatoes off his head
for good.

"So," Aladdin said, "what's this about
saving the kingdom?"

"I was just kidding around," Iago said
quickly. "You know me. Such a kidder."
He pointed to Jahmad's plans. "You really
figure I can do this nice thing, huh?"

"Sure." Aladdin smiled. "I've always kind
of suspected that beneath your rotten exte-
rior beats a heart of gold." He hesitated.
"Well, silver, anyway."

It's more like concrete, said the annoying
little voice in Iago's head as he flew away
without another word.

"Look at all the people!" the Sultan exclaimed from the palace balcony. "Everyone in Agrabah is here for the fireworks!"

On the grounds in front of the palace, a huge crowd had gathered. The sun had just begun to set behind the dunes beyond the city, turning the sky to fire.

"Can we get this show on the road already?" Iago demanded.

"Iago!" Jasmine said. "You've sure been on edge this evening."

"The sooner we do the fireworks thing,

the sooner I can stop being nice and get my birdbath."

"Too bad your time is almost up," Aladdin said. "I was getting used to the peace and quiet."

"You won't have peace and quiet for long," said the Sultan. "Not after the fireworks start!" He peered into the big container of fireworks that the guards had brought out. "That's strange," he said. "I could have sworn we had more fireworks last year." He turned to one of the palace guards. "Are you sure this is all we have in the storage room?"

"Yes, Your Highness," said the guard. "That's everything."

Iago glanced at the half-empty container. He knew where the other fireworks were — with Sargon and Jahmad.

Tell them, said the little voice in his head.

"No, you moron," Iago muttered. "I'm just a few minutes away from my birdbath."

"What did you say?" Aladdin asked.

"Who, me? Nothing," Iago said quickly. "Just talking to myself."

"Aladdin, Jasmine, make a note," said the Sultan. "Next year, remind me to order more fireworks. I like *lots* of noise."

The Genie appeared on the balcony, holding dozens of sparklers between his fingers and toes. He whirled around like a pinwheel, making a blazing circle of sparkling light.

"Excellent, Genie, excellent!" the Sultan exclaimed.

The Genie collapsed in a dizzy heap. "Do me a favor, Al," he said. "Make the palace stop spinning."

Iago paced back and forth nervously. "Isn't it time yet?"

"We have to wait until dark," Aladdin reminded him.

"Don't worry, Iago," said the Sultan. "That birdbath is going to be yours after all."

"Who'd have guessed he could be such a sweetheart?" Jasmine said. She gave Iago a pat on the head.

"Iago's a good egg," the Genie agreed. "Come to think of it, he used to *be* an egg."

Iago perched on the balcony railing and stared out at the crowd. He didn't want people saying nice things about him. He was not a good egg. He was more the hard-boiled, rotten variety.

A movement near the edge of the crowd caught his eye. Two men were leading a

camel toward the back of the palace. Two very familiar men — Sargon and Jahmad.

Iago watched them. They would have no trouble getting past the other guards. After all, Sargon was in charge. He was trusted.

Just like Aladdin and Jasmine and the Sultan trust you, said that annoying voice.

"Would you can it already?" Iago growled.

"What was that, Iago?" Jasmine asked.

"Nothing, Princess." Iago sighed. "I was just saying there's something I've gotta check out. I'll be right back."

"But the fireworks are about to start!" the Sultan cried.

"You don't know the half of it," Iago said grimly.

Iago flew around to the back of the palace.
No guards were in sight. The camel was
standing near one of the back doors. There
were two large empty pouches on his back.

Carefully Iago peered through the open
doorway. Just as he'd suspected, Sargon
and Jahmad were heading down the stairs
to the treasure room. Jahmad was carrying
his toolbox. Inside, Iago knew, were the
stolen fireworks.

KA-BOOM! Suddenly the first fireworks
of the evening went off on the other side of

the palace. Iago could hear the crowd cheering at the cascade of colorful sparks.

A moment later Jahmad and Sargon ran from the stairwell. They dashed down the hall and threw themselves to the floor, covering their ears.

KA-BOOM!!! Iago leaped in the air. This time the explosion was earsplitting. Smoke and bits of wood filled the air. The fireworks had blown the treasure room door right off its hinges.

Sargon and Jahmad got up and dusted themselves off. "That was easier than I thought it would be," said Sargon. "It required only a few of the fireworks. Now the fun begins! Go get the pouches off the camel."

Iago hid near the door, watching as Jahmad grabbed the pouches and disappeared down the stairs leading to the treasure room.

A few minutes later Jahmad returned. This time he was struggling under the weight of the filled pouches. Each was

stuffed to the brim with jewels that glinted in the moonlight.

Sargon joined Jahmad. "There's so much more left!" he whined. "How can we carry it all?"

"We can put more loot in my toolbox," Jahmad said. "We'll dump the extra fireworks out. There will be plenty of room."

"Talk about greedy," Iago muttered as the two men hurried back down the stairs. "They're taking everything they can get their grimy hands on."

He considered going to get Aladdin. But it was a little late for that. By the time Iago explained everything, Jahmad and Sargon would be long gone with the treasure.

On the other hand, if Iago saved the day on his own, he wouldn't have broken his promise not to say anything mean about anyone. *And* he'd get bonus points for thwarting a jewel heist.

That would mean an extra-big birdbath. Birdbath! Suddenly Iago had an idea.

He waited until Sargon and Jahmad returned, dragging the toolbox filled with jewels. While they began to secure the box on the camel's back, Iago sneaked down to the treasure room. He found the spot where Sargon and Jahmad had dumped the extra fireworks. Iago selected the biggest firecracker in the pile and grabbed it.

By the time Iago got outside, Jahmad and Sargon were leading the camel through the palace gardens toward the back gate. In the front the crowd still roared as the fireworks display lit up the sky. The air rolled with thunderous booms and whistles as the fireworks soared through the sky.

As he struggled to fly with the heavy firecracker, Iago looked around. He spotted a torch burning near the fountain in the center of the gardens. He flew over and carefully lit the fuse of the firecracker. The wick sizzled and began to burn.

"If I don't hurry," Iago muttered, "I am going to go out with a bang. A big bang. We're talking pureed parrot."

With the burning firecracker clutched in

his claws, Iago flew to Abu's favorite palm
tree. He perched on one of the branches
and looked down. Sargon and Jahmad
were hurrying down the path that led
straight past Iago's birdbath.

Iago glanced down at the firecracker he
was holding and gulped nervously. The
wick was more than half burned. "Hurry
up, you creeps," he muttered.

"I'll go ahead to see if the coast is clear,"
Sargon told Jahmad. "You wait here."

Sargon ran off. The wick sizzled. Just
another inch and the firecracker would go
off with a bang. If Iago didn't get rid of it
quickly, *he'd* be going off with a bang, too.

There was only one thing to do. Iago cleared his throat. "Oh, Jahmad!" he called in a perfect imitation of Sargon's voice.

"Wh-where are you?" Jahmad asked. "I thought you were going to see if the coast was clear."

"Over here, next to the birdbath," Iago called in Sargon's voice. "Bring the camel. And hurry!"

Stumbling in the darkness, Jahmad made his way toward the birdbath.

"If that mangy monkey can do it, so can I," Iago whispered, taking aim. "Five . . . four . . . three . . . two . . . one . . ."

As the last bit of wick sizzled, Iago let the firecracker go. It sailed downward. Iago crossed his wings hopefully.

KA-BLOOEY!!!

Just as it landed in a pouch full of jewels, the firecracker went off in a huge explosion of red, blue, and yellow sparks. The sky was filled with color. Suddenly Iago realized it wasn't just the explosion he was seeing — it was the Sultan's jewels, flying into the air!

The camel reared up, dumping the remaining jewels on the ground, and ran for cover. Jahmad lay on the ground, his ears covered, as diamonds and rubies and emeralds fell like rain.

Sargon came running back. "What have you done?" he cried. "Our jewels! They're everywhere, you fool!"

"But it wasn't my fault!" Jahmad sobbed. "An explosion came down on me from the sky. I swear it is true."

Sargon looked up. Iago looked down. He gave a little wave. "Hi, guys. Sorry to ruin your party."

Sargon spluttered and shook his fist at the parrot. Then he dropped to his knees, scrabbling frantically for the scattered jewels.

"Not so fast, bud," Iago said. "I nearly toasted my tail over those jewels." He flew down, trying to stop Jahmad and Sargon from picking up any more of the treasure.

Jahmad pointed. "The . . . the Sultan's guards are coming!" he cried. "We must run, Sargon!"

"Just one more diamond," Sargon said.

"I don't think so, Sargon," Aladdin called.

"Stop where you are!" Jasmine yelled. "Surround them, guards!"

In a flash of glinting swords, Iago, Jahmad, and Sargon were instantly circled by guards.

Jasmine and Aladdin stared at the

strange sight before them. The Sultan's jewels were spread around the gardens like drops of shining dew. Jahmad and Sargon lay cowering on the ground, their hands and pockets filled with treasure.

Meanwhile, Abu had arrived and was busy scooping up every jewel he could find and depositing them in his fez.

Aladdin crossed his arms over his chest. "Let's see," he said. "Who wants to go first?"

"That crazy parrot tried to blow us up!" Sargon cried.

"Perhaps he tried to blow you up because you were stealing the Sultan's treasure," Aladdin said.

"No, no, it was him," Sargon said quickly. "The bird was the one who tried to steal the treasure! We caught him. You must believe me!"

"Forget it, Sargon," Jasmine said. "We caught you red-handed. And it all fits together. Rasoul's accident, you volunteering to guard the treasure room. . . . We should have seen it ourselves. But we were too busy with the Ceremony of Fireworks to pay attention. We're just lucky Iago *was* paying attention." She walked over to Iago and gave him a kiss on the head. "The Genie's right. You really are a good egg, Iago. Loud mouth and all."

"Am I blushing or what?" Iago said happily. "Tell me the truth."

"The first thing we need to do is gather up all the Sultan's treasure," Aladdin said. "Guards, take Sargon and Jahmad away. We'll worry about their punishment later." He winked at Iago. "But I'm thinking they could start with a building project."

"Say, maybe a birdbath?" Iago asked.

"You read my mind," Aladdin said.

"Am I now officially free to be me again?" Iago asked.

"Yes, Iago," Aladdin said, smiling. "Unfortunately."

"Good," Iago said. He smiled sweetly at Abu. "Drop the jewels, monkey boy! It's no more Mr. Nice Parrot!"

Abu's eyes went wide. He scampered up the palm tree as fast as he could, with Iago on his tail.

"You're mine, you flea farm! You over-size rat! You rotten, smelly little ape! Mine, at long last!" Iago screeched.

Jasmine watched the chase with a smile. "Well," she said to Aladdin, "he may have a heart of gold, but his *mouth* is pure tin!"